D1203780

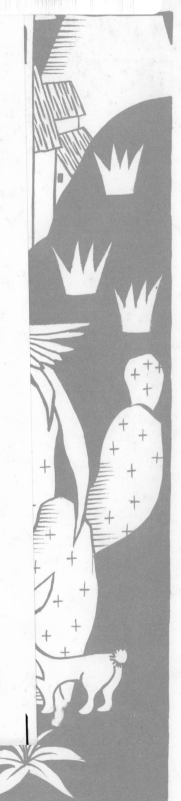

Chiquitico, the least one, a burrito the color of soft gray clouds, was, thought Paco, the most beautiful, the most to be desired of all the burros in Mexico.

"Soft and gray and good-for-nothing," said Vicente.

"You two," he would . y, "a son and a burrito to make the stomach ill. You make a day's work out of nothing at all. You blow yourselves away in the morning like smoke, and get yourselves blown back again at night to fill your stomachs, the better to idle tomorrow. Four idle hoofs, two worthless legs, two empty heads—puf!"

"Thou art right, always, papacito," agreed Paco.

But later, on the hillside, he would whisper into one of the least one's ears:

"Burrito, it is something to belong to ourselves alone—and to each other. The world will get hold of us soon enough, but now it is good.

"Look at the Zopilotes overhead. We are free as they are, and they are the freest creatures in all God's sky—on all of God's earth. Who is to tell them whither to go, whence to come? Who is to molest them? They are the kings of the air as we are the kings of today and this hillside. Ohu, it is a good feeling."

One day, however, Vicente laid the burden cloth upon the least one's back, and sent Paco to the fábrica to apprentice himself to the sandal-maker. And on that evening, Chiquitico did not come home and might not have been seen again, except that the good San Francisco, patron saint of animals, must have realized how important boy and burro were to each other.

THE VIKING PRESS
18 EAST 48TH STREET
NEW YORK CITY

0912

THE LEAST ONE

Also by Ruth Sawyer

THE
LEAST ONE

BY RUTH SAWYER

ILLUSTRATED BY LEO POLITI

THE VIKING PRESS · NEW YORK · 1941

STATE STREET METHODIST CHURCH LIBRARY
BRISTOL, PENNA.

FIRST PUBLISHED OCTOBER 1941

SECOND PRINTING AUGUST 1943

THIRD PRINTING MARCH 1945

FOURTH PRINTING OCTOBER 1947

FIFTH PRINTING AUGUST 1950

SIXTH PRINTING NOVEMBER 1953

COPYRIGHT 1941 BY RUTH SAWYER

PRINTED IN U. S. A. BY REEHL LITHO COMPANY

PUBLISHED ON THE SAME DAY IN THE DOMINION OF CANADA BY

THE MACMILLAN COMPANY OF CANADA LIMITED

To Beetle

STATE STREET METHODIST CHURCH LIBRARY
BRISTOL, VIRGINIA

William N. Neff Center
For Teacher Education
Emory & Henry College
Emory, Virginia 24327

WITHDRAWN

SMALL, LITTLE, AND LEAST

CHICO was the small one—the color of dull slate and a good burro to work. Vicente, his master, loved him above all burros and pointed to him always with pride. "Look, there is no load too big for that one. He will carry anything."

Chiquita was little—the color of the brown pottery she carried every Friday to market. Vicente said she was not too bad, not for a little burro. She would carry almost half her weight in jugs and bowls, or firewood, up the twisting streets, her tiny polished hoofs never slipping on the worn cobbles. "And when I twist her tail to make her move faster, does she kick or bite?" Vicente would ask. "No! Only a squeal comes out of her."

Chiquitico was the least one—the color of those soft gray clouds with white edges that the winds blow over the top of Popocatepetl like puffs of thistle-down. "Soft and gray and good-for-nothing," said Vicente.

Paco, who was small himself, and not good for very much, pointed out with delight that the three burros grew smaller as their names

9

grew longer, that as their names grew longer they grew more beautiful and to be desired. Which made Chiquitico the most beautiful, the most to be desired of all burros in Mexico. And that is saying a great deal. For the burros of Mexico are as many as the stars and beyond all counting.

Chiquitico was the youngest as well as the least, a son born to the small and the little one. First Paco had counted his age in days, then in weeks, by notching the bark on the papaya trunk with Vicente's machete. Now he counted it by the new crescent moons. Soon the least one would be a year old, and soon—far too soon—Vicente would be thinking about putting the burden cloth upon him and making him into a pack-burro like Chico and Chiquita. That would be a terrible day; and although Paco hated with all his might to let the thought of it slip into his mind at all, slip it did. From his mind it went down into the very depths of his stomach, making him ache all the way upwards to his ears. For when that terrible day came to pass, gone would be the hours of delight spent together.

Paco knew that no burro who carried loads all day had any lightness left in small hoofs to climb down the steep sides of the barrancas, to skim over the hard-packed plains, to follow the goat-paths up the mountains to where the pines stood thick for shade and smelled cool and spicy. Boy and burro—they would never again be free after the burden cloth had once been laid across the least one.

Vicente was a carrier. Wherever there was a load to be carried from this place to that there he was with his burros. And three would carry more than two. More loads—more money—more to eat. There were bags of maize to be carried to the mill; there were bags of charcoal to be carried down from the mountain; there was pottery to be fetched to market, and wherever there was a new house building or an old one repaired, there were tiles to be carried up from the kiln. Never an idle day but Sunday for Vicente, the small one and the little one.

But for Paco and the least one there were many idle days. In all of Mexico, so said Vicente, there were no greater idlers—idlers and good-for-nothings. The words were on his tongue whenever he had time to take his eyes from his work and rest them upon Paco and Chiquitico. "You two," he would say, "a son and a burrito to make the stomach ill. You make a day's work out of nothing at all. You blow yourselves away in the morning like smoke, and get yourselves blown back again at night to fill your stomachs, the better to idle tomorrow. Four idle hoofs, two worthless legs, two empty heads—puf!"

And Paco, always thinking of the enchanting places where those hoofs and legs had transported them, of the contentment and dreams that had filled at least one of the empty heads, sighed and shrugged his shoulders and did his best to agree with his father as he should. "Thou art right, always, papacito. But we molest no one. That is something."

"That is on the under side of nothing. A pity I have not a son worthy of the name I have given him and of the food that he has been eating for ten good years. Or is it eleven?"

"I have lost count." Paco said it wearily. But always when Vicente had gone he would whisper into one of the least one's ears: "Let the papá think what he likes. It eases his stomach. But we know it is enough to be the best burro in all Mexico, in the Atlantic and the Pacific Oceans, in the United States of America, and in the family of Vicente Rabell. And some day the good San Francisco will bless thee, least of all burros."

Paco never knew why he was always talking about this blessing business. The old Spanish custom of blessing all creatures on the Day of San Francisco had long been abandoned in Mexico. The ancient ones still talked about it, but for himself, it had never happened within his remembrance. Never had he taken part, nor had any of the burros

taken part, in a fiesta for that good saint who watched over them. But it was something that Paco kept always in one pocket of his mind, to draw out secretly and show only to Chiquitico. It was one of the very important matters that passed between them when they were at rest on the foot-hills, beyond reach of all calling. The boy talked of it; the least one listened so intently that no one could have doubted but that he laid as great importance on it as did Paco. And why shouldn't he, for it concerned him, absolutamente! For if good San Francisco could bless the least one, then in some miraculous way thenceforth he might be safe from all heavy burdens: never become a pack-burro, never wear the burden cloth, never have his back chafed raw for a thousand flies to molest!

Pleasant days, and most of the days were pleasant, Paco and the least one climbed or idled as the spirit willed. The lonely barrancas and hill-sides knew them; the plowed fields and the farmers knew them; the forests and the charcoal burners knew them. They made, boy and burro, good listeners beside the pits while the men waited for the stout trees they had felled to char, to be uncovered, cooled, bagged, and made ready for carrying. They knew good stories to tell, those charcoal burners, and Paco and the least one liked to listen.

One day the big carbonero, Justino Pacheco, told a tale of three burros.

"Were they small, little, and least?" asked Paco.

"The tale does not tell, but thou shalt have them so."

"Vaya contar—go on with the telling," said the other men.

"Very well. There were three burros; all there was in the way of a family for one boy."

"His name?"

"That does not matter."

"I can think of the tale better if the boy has a name. It is not good—not to be named."

"All right. The name shall be Rufino. This Rufino now, one day he let his fire go out. Then how could he cook the tortillas, how, the beans? So he went to borrow fire from the old witch on the mountain. That was not good. To borrow fire from anyone puts you into their power, as all know. So she gives Rufino a burning fagot and seeds; she tells him to plant the seeds about his hut. They will grow into good vegetables. He took the fire; he took the seeds. He made himself a fresh hearth-burning; he planted the seeds. Next morning they were full grown; the burros ate of them, and puf!"

"Puf—what?"

"They were gone. The witch had cast a spell upon them. Every burro turned into a zopilote and flew away."

Paco swallowed hard. "Could he never get them back, that Rufino, not even the least one?"

"He could and he did. But by hard work and many days. He traveled over three rivers, one of fire, one of frost, and one of flood. This river was blessed, the water was holy. He brought back enough in his cap, and when the zopilotes flew close he sprinkled their tails. Then they became burros again, but burros of skin and bone, for the witch had worked them almost to death, while he was gone."

"Are there witches—many?"

"Who knows? Not until you hear one say 'Without God and Mary,' and fly off into the night can you tell she is a witch."

"I don't like them—witches," said Paco. "I hope they stay away from our village."

On gala days the men in the market place knew them, the women too. There Paco had a wheedling tongue for a handful of espinaca for Chiquitico—spinach to any American donkey; and for himself he could wheedle a handful of sugared squash-seeds, or some sweetmeat. He showed the men respect and the women flattery. He made good trade for them among the tourists, and he taught the least one the trick of bobbing a "good day" to all.

But for both, these wanderings meant something more than lazy days and succulent morsels. Neither could have told what it was that brought so many hurtling moments of joy, that sent their hearts capering ahead of their legs. Often when the two were alone, the burro grazing on whatever was at hand convenient for foraging, Paco lying on his back, knees erect and hands lifting his head, slightly tilted, for a wider view of the two snow-capped volcanoes in the distance, there would come bubbling up from the depths of the boy's fancy, words that had to be spoken aloud so that both he and the least one might savor them together. Then it was of many things he would talk.

"The volcanoes now, thou gray one, they are the presidentes over all the little hills, the barrancas, the plains, the forests. They rule them well, and when they do not obey one or the other of them—Popo or Ixty—spits fire at them. That frightens them and they behave.

"Burrito, it is something to belong to ourselves alone—and to each other. The world will get hold of us soon enough, but now it is good. Look at the zopilotes overhead. We are as free as they are, and they are the freest creatures in all of God's sky—on all of God's earth. Who is to tell them whither to go, whence to come? Who is to molest them? They are the kings of the air as we are the kings of today and this hillside. Ohu, it is a good feeling."

Now the small, the little, and the least ones lived outside the jacal of Vicente. With them lived a black pig with brown patches, and a whitish pig with black patches, and a pig that was pink all over. Every pig was for himself; but there were seven goats who were friendly, who talked a great deal to one another and to anyone who cared to listen. There was, as well, a turkey, a rooster, three hens, and a fluttering of pigeons. The pigeons made a pleasant sound, coming and going; they nested under the palm-thatch of the jacal. Below, in the nearest barranca, which held a fast-running stream when the rains fell in the spring, there lived an ancient, fat green frog. He lived strictly alone, and Paco called him el soltero—the bachelor.

The jacal was a hut made of slender bamboo trunks thrust deep into the clayish earth when the earth was wet. The clay dried, the sun fired it firm, and there they stood, fast and strong and able to hold up the heavily thatched roof. The jacal was almost square, not too large and not too small. In front the thatch came down well over the doorway, like the visor of a soldier's cap, making a shady sitting place outside the hut. From nails in the bamboo, in zigzag rows across the hut, hung gourds and earthen pots holding growing plants. Some were always in flower, and Paco thought it was the prettiest home on all the hillside. Back of it stood a high, wide-spreading jacaranda tree. Its leaves were as feathery as the open wing of a pigeon, and its blossoms so blue that Paco liked to think that the tree picked fresh ones every morning from the sky. A big old banana tree that no longer bore fruit stood in the yard and gave shade to fine dusting holes for the hens and rooster. Straight in front of the hut shot up a papaya tree. All the year round it bore fruit that was succulent as a melon and when cracked open as ripe and yellow as the sun. There was one thing more growing outside of

Vicente's jacal—that was a great bush of angels' trumpets. The blossoms as white as the peak of Popocatepetl.

"It is the prettiest jacal in all the world," Paco would think to himself, boastfully, as he ran spry-legged up or down the hill, always stopping midway to admire it. "Chiquitico is the most beautiful of all the burritos." And then, because Mexican children are very loyal to their own: "I have a nice papá and a nice mamá, and the ups-and-downs are as good as any."

The ups were older and the downs were younger than he was. Altogether when Rosa, their mother, called them they became: "José-Ana-Claudio-Paco-Felipe-Juanita-Rafael-come-here!"

Under the thatched visor of the hut there was a table and bench and stools. Inside Rosa prepared the meals, but outside they were eaten except on late evenings when it was too cold. It was pleasant to sit there, sheltered from sun or wind, watching the world go by, listening to Vicente tell of the day's adventures. He was a good carrier, that Vicente, to remember and carry home the smallest piece of news that he had picked up on the road or at market or in the Zócalo.

Inside the hut the floor was packed so hard that Rosa could sweep it with a broom. At night, curled up in two allotted corners on the floor, slept the ups-and-downs on dried cane-leaves, which made warm, dry beds, with a serape to throw over them. On cold nights they would huddle like puppies together; on warm nights they would scatter.

In one corner slept Vicente and Rosa on a fine matrimonio, the only bed on legs in the hut. Over it was nailed a shelf just large enough to hold a picture of the Holy Mother, and a short fat candle that burned all night long. Kneeling on the matrimonio, every one of the ups-and-downs—except Rafael, who could not yet walk—said his evening

prayers before scuttling to the corner. They did not wash, they did not undress, but they never forgot to pray. Always they reminded the Holy Mother that the candle was for Her, never forgotten. Always they supplicated Her to watch over them through the night and bring them safely and contentedly to another day, not overlooking Rafael, who could not make his own supplications.

Over the doorway, which possessed no door, at night was hung a thick-woven serape to keep out the wind, should it blow too fiercely, and the cold, and the rains—when they came. It also kept out whatever prowling dogs and men might be about; at least it did as a rule. But the family were never too surprised to wake in the morning to find a stranger or a stray dog added to the huddle of children in the corners. For who were they to deny shelter at night to a wanderer? And was not all safe with the candle burning? They would have gone without maize for the good tortillas, without beans and without chile, they would have gone hungry to bed without a whimper rather than sleep without a candle to burn to the Holy Mother, the mother of all sorrows, all joys, all papás and mamás and ups-and-downs.

It was nice to lie, eyes stretched wide, to watch the tiny, pointed flame rising, always rising toward this Mother of All, rising even as their prayers. It was nice to wet a finger and hold it aloft to feel whatever breeze might be sifting through the chinks of the bamboo, to smell the sweet, pungent smell of burning wax. Ohu, it was good to let eyelids that had grown too heavy close, knowing one was so well guarded.

But sometimes, when the night was still and close, Paco would slip his serape over his head, lift the serape at the door, and steal out into the night, exchanging the guardianship of the candle for the companionship of the least one. He would feel his way with his bare, brown feet across the yard to the edge of the barranca where the least one always found his hollow for resting. He would call ahead his coming in soft, endearing sounds and the burrito would answer him with a sound that was not a whinny or a bray but a nurseling's call of delight. In another moment Paco would be lying in the hollow, close to the gray-and-whiteness. His heart would be beating like a dance-drum with a strange night happiness that was unlike any contentment that came by day. He would pillow his head on the cushiony side of the burrito and feel the least one's heart beating faster than his own. He would cup his small, square brown hand over the softest muzzle to feel the least one's nuzzling breath.

Ohu! It was good to lie so under the great roof of the sky, to share heart-beats, to have not one candle but thousands to light one's prayers heavenwards. Without doubt, he had a good papá and mamá—sin duda—and the ups-and-downs were all that the middling one could ask. But Chiquitico was his. With eyes blinded he could have picked the least one out of all the burros in Mexico, shape of ears, wetness of muzzle, silky-softness of hair. To keep the least one always his he would have given Vicente, Rosa, the ups-and-downs, all three pigs, all seven goats—the rooster— Puf! What would he not have given!

In a little while the heartbeats of boy and burro would quiet; the night-peace would cover them with the lightness of slow-running water. Thoughts in great abundance would crowd Paco's mind, and words would fit themselves to the thoughts. These words he would always speak aloud to the least one. "Listen, burrito," he would whisper, "it is there that they all live, the Holy Ones, behind the stars. There is the Good God, the Blessed Mother, the Gentle Jesus, and all the saints. To me belongs the Good God, I think, and the Blessed

Mother. I am not sure about the Gentle Jesus. He may belong to burritos as well as boys. But this I know for a great certainty—San Francisco is thy saint as well as mine. Always remember that."

One night, having admonished the least one, he let his fancies rush
back to the sky overhead. "I am always wondering why they do not
drop down on us, those Holy Ones from up there. They must be fastened in tighter than the stars. Often I have seen the stars fall to earth.
On summer nights I have counted as many as two handfuls in a single
night. Once the great chandelier in the cathedral fell. It had been up in
the ceiling for over a hundred years when the fastenings gave way after
an earthquake and down it came. I am always wondering why the
earthquakes do not shake down the Holy Ones. Fastenings cannot last
forever."

The possibilities of this idea started Paco's heart to beating very fast.
With a sudden surge of feeling he sat erect, beginning to shiver all over
like the leaves on the jacaranda. He looked into the soft adoring eyes
of the least one, then back to the heavens. He panted with excitement,
his fingers taking the direction his eyes had already taken. "Magnifico!" It scraped the lining of his stomach to think about it: the
fastenings giving way—the Holy Ones falling to earth—to walk the
highroads, the streets—to be seen, without doubt, talking together in
the Zócalo—that park where everybody gathered and talked—to be
one with the tourists. "Magnifico!"

Chiquitico must have felt it to be magnificent. He sprang suddenly
to his small hoofs, standing sharply outlined on the ridge of the barranca, shaking, too, like the leaves of the jacaranda. Paco went on,
throwing words at him: "They would not all come together—prob-
ablemente. They would drop like the stars, one at a time, some falling

to this place, some to another. We could not expect to get all of them in this village. The Blessed Mother would, perhaps, come here. She would call us by our names. She would know us all because of our prayers. She would stand at the doorways of our jacals and look inside at dusk and see the candles burning and know us. Ohu—wonderful! And the dust upon the roads would not touch Her garments as She passed.

"God, I think, would not drop. He would have a special fastening that would last forever and ever. But the Gentle Jesus, now, He might come to the Zócalo. He might stand under the big ahuehuete tree, teaching the little children, laying the hands upon them. Luisa would bring her last baby, who is blind. Old Tito would come on his half legs and see could the Gentle Jesus pull them out at the stumps and make whole ones of them."

Paco was kneeling now, in a great reverence for his thoughts. Where had they come from? Amazing; he had begun with the stars which he could see overhead and had ended with a miracle taking place in his very own village and which he couldn't see at all. He sat back on his feet and silently let his thoughts run away into a confused distance, where nothing was very clear. When they came back, it was with a leap. Let the Holy Ones fall where they would. Let only San Francisco, the burrito's saint and his, fall upon them. Then truly would the blessing be assured.

The least one was overcome. He sank to his knees, rolled to his side, his back, and there he rocked, like a ship in the trough of the sea, four wisps of legs like masts straight in the air. Then, as suddenly, he scrambled to his feet, dislodging many stones, sending them rattling down the side of the barranca. One moment he paused. Paco watched him as if both had come under a spell. Then the least one raised his muzzle and gave forth the lusty, long blasting bray of a full-grown burro. It was his first, and it shot him off up the hillside, into the night, leaving the boy alone.

Paco sat stark and stiff. That bray! What if the papá had heard it! An instant and he was on his knees, his hands raised in supplication: "María mía, let him snore his ears shut that he may hear nothing, think nothing."

THE LEAST ONE VANISHES

THE family of Vicente was astir early that morning. Vicente had an order to carry many tiles far up on the hillside to a place where a house was building for the American artist. It was to be a carmen, a summer house with garden. If he, Vicente, carried full loads and fast, there might be days of work ahead. The builder was a friend. This was hard work. Three burros would be better than two. He came out of the hut to wash his face in the one pool the dry seasons always left in the barranca, and unseen he came upon Paco and the least one.

Paco had risen earlier than the rest of the family. He wanted to make sure the least one had returned. Finding him covered with brush, his fetlocks and tail matted with spines, he had secured the family comb and was absorbed in restoring perfection to Chiquitico. He had gotten out all the spines and was now occupied in making the hair stand out all over the burro like a very puffy cloud. He was also chanting an old Indian tune and putting words he liked to it:

> Ohu—least one.
> Thy hoofs are small as brown snails,
> But thou art fleet as the deer,
> As the deer into the night thou canst lose thyself.
> The eyes are round and bright as the berries on the ash tree.
> They are as bright as the morning star over Popo.
> Under the hairs of thy hide and under my brown skin
> We are brothers, least one,
> And each knows what the other is thinking.

"Thinking!" shouted Vicente like an angry man. "That is all the two of you are good for—thinking. I will tell you what you think—that every day is a fiesta and that the business of filling nine mouths is as easy as pitching stones at the moon."

Paco stood, himself filled with fear, while he marked the anger rising in his father. Ordinarily Vicente was a patient man; no one knew this better than his children. But when once his anger started there was no quelling it, as there was no quelling the rising waters in the barranca when the spring rains came. One watched and did nothing, and in time they receded and all was peaceful again. This Paco was thinking. If he could but take the brunt of this anger and spare the least one.

"Papá, it is all true what thou sayest of me, all true. I am a good-for-nothing. But do not say it of the least of all burritos, not this one, please——"

Vicente cut him short. "Call him no longer a burrito. Did I not hear him bray last night? Fool thyself no longer. You will both become men

today and quit this business of thinking. Thou shalt get thyself to the fábrica and apprentice thyself to Manuel Juárez, the sandal-maker. But first thou shalt put the burden cloth on Chiquitico. Today I intend to make him think tiles upon his back. Many tiles!"

With a heart that not only sank but slowly went to pieces at the bottom of his stomach, Paco did as his father had told him. Whispering caution in the least one's ear: "Thou shalt mind the papá well and quickly that he may not twist thy tail. Oh, best of all burros, I could not stand to live and have him twist thy tail."

He watched the least one follow Chico and Chiquita out through the bamboo gate into the road, the burrito looking curiously behind him, expecting Paco to follow. All three burros were plainly interested in this new departure. Mother and father looked at their offspring with inquiring glances, stopped to nuzzle him, only to jump forward at Vicente's command and take the lead again.

The last Paco saw was the look of despair in the least one's eyes, the urgent cocking of the ears, the annoyed slash of the tail when Paco did not move his weight from the cross-bar of the gate and follow. When all had disappeared, slowly, with feet that could hardly be lifted, the boy took a second road, leading down to the center of the town. He came to the Zócalo; from there, by a cross-street, to the shop of the sandal-maker. Within, in sheds built about the patio, the business of converting goat-hides into many-colored sandals went on all day long. A green and yellow parrot hung outside, uncaged but on a perch. He remarked on Paco's coming with a shrill chuckle and said in perfect English: "What—here's another!"

Paco did not understand but he resented the parrot's tone. He resented being there at all; he resented life itself. Why should he live? This business of becoming a man overnight held no joy for him. To sit inside the fábrica, a place where the winds could not blow down one's lavender shirt or up one's cotton pants, a place where the roof of heaven was chopped off into a small square no bigger than a kerchief; to learn how to soak goat-hides in a vat, puf—that was a stinking business! He might as well be dead.

Every minute of that day was terrible. It had a hundred hours. He might have arms and legs to do the patron's bidding, but his mind was not on goat but on one burro. He could think of nothing but the least one. All day long he thought: "I hope papá is patient. I hope he remembers that this is Chiquitico's first day, that no burrito can be made in one day into an old pack animal. Papá—papacito—the tiles are heavy. Do not put too many on his back at one time!" Throughout the day his lips moved in silent supplication.

Unforunately Vicente could not hear it. He carried his anger still with him. This business of being a carrier was serious. The village had many carriers, too many. To keep always at work meant to keep moving, to carry good loads, to be cheerful, and to deliver the cargo safely.

At the kiln Vicente gave to the small one and the little one their usual loadings, as much as they could stagger under and still keep their balance. Then he gave all his attention to the least one, speaking aloud what was in his mind: "We will have no foolishness. Thou didst bray like a full-sized burro; we will give thee a full-sized load." Which he did. One thickness of tiles might have served well for a first carrying, but Vicente packed them in double rows, fastening the canvas straps relentlessly about the least one's middle.

A word sufficed to the two—Chico and Chiquita—to start them up the sharp climb. But to the least one he gave more; he spanked him smartly across the flanks, which made him jump, shaking with amazement and anger. No one had ever struck him before. Stock still he stood, so covered with tiles that all one could see of him was a pair of ears, four fragile legs, and an angry tail that lashed rebelliously.

"So thou canst be a stubborn burro as well as a good-for-nothing. We shall see." Whereupon Vicente's hand fell again, harder this time.

Slowly, under a weight that must have seemed to him no less than the whole earth, Chiquitico moved up the steep road. But he moved only when Vicente insisted with the flat of his hand. It was slow— slow—slow. It took all the nagging, the spanking, the unspeakable language that Vicente could use to keep the least one in motion. The small and the little ones were fast outdistancing them. They were up and over the second dip of the road before the least one had barely put his feet to the road at all.

"Is it a month or a year we take to deliver the first load?" Vicente inquired of the ears now set flat to the head. "Is it a burro thou art or a snail? Is this a joke we are fooling ourselves with, or is it a matter of silver, a tostón for each full loading? Answer me that? Look ahead at thy father and thy mother and get into thy wooden head how it is a good burro works for his master."

So went the climbing. Words-words-words followed by spanks-spanks-spanks. Never had Vicente gone at so slow a pace, never had he been so hot, so breathless, so downpouring with sweat. He marked the spot that would be half-way to the carmen. Then he marked the time by the sun overhead; then he grew angrier than ever. "Estúpido! At this rate it will be nightfall when we reach the top. We will try a different cure for thy ailment." He reached for the tail of the least one and gave it a quick, strong twist.

Now, to be a burro and to have one's tail twisted is to suffer a hurt so great that it is beyond all telling. For an instant it paralyzed the least one. Then he gave a squeal so pitiful that it would have melted the earth itself. The next instant, being on the edge of the road, he lost his balance and turned twice, completely over, landing in a ditch below. There he lay on his back, four legs sticking straight upwards in the air.

It was Vicente's turn to be paralyzed. To have a stubborn burro that rolled himself into a ditch was unheard of, not to be believed. "Pity more than nothing!" he shouted as he almost rolled himself down after the burro into the ditch. At the foot of the bank he stood and looked to see how many tiles might be broken. He would have to replace every one. Not a sound came from Chiquitico; many words, and not of a politeness, came from Vicente. He felt the pack over. Nearly a good half the load, or a bad half, was broken. Maldiciones, curses, on such a creature. His anger shook him like a tempest wind. For the first time in his life, Vicente wished evil on another.

"May thou be thrice cursed! Through thy height, thy width, thy thickness may thou turn into a wooden burro, good for nothing but to stand still the rest of thy stupid, worthless life!" he shouted.

With a jerk of his mind he remembered the small and little ones, by this time nearing the carmen. He must hasten after them or they might think they were tired and lie down on their packs, and more tiles would have to be paid for. Pronto, he must make a safe delivery. Mumbling something about leaving the small gray rascal to do a penance for his stubbornness, Vicente hurried up the road.

But the weight of the curse he carried with him and a kind of horror. Anxiously he scanned the heavens overhead for any bird on the wing to carry that curse from him. All good Mexicans know that a bird flying may bear an idle curse away, keep it from falling, especially if one says to the bird: "Take it in Mary's name." But there was no bird in the sky. Vicente made slits of his eyes the better to see afar, and not a wing, anywhere, clipped the air. That was bad; that was a calamity.

What would the good padre think; what would Rosa think! Did not the church warn against such evil mouthings? He would take the curse back and he would never think of it again. Por Dios, he was a sinner. Not fit to be the proud master of three good burros and the father of seven ups-and-downs. He would light a candle on the Sunday coming, to burn away the blackness of that sin he had committed in great anger. Aí—better to pay for half a load of broken tiles and a candle than to blacken one's soul.

The long day for Paco ended at last. At last the apprentices gave the hides in the vats one more turn about, swept the slicings of leather from the floor, put away tools and benches, and hung up the finished sandals in one of the many rows which ran around the fábrica, tier on tier. That first awful day was done.

Paco stepped into the cool, fresh air of the streets and wiped the stink of goat from his nose with a violent rubbing of his sleeve. Now, this very moment, the papá might be home, and the small, the little, and the least ones with him. Ehu! From now on Chiquitico might belong to Vicente throughout the day, but no one could take away his belonging to him, Paco, at the day's end. They would share the good nights together, the stars overhead, the talk about the Holy Ones, and above all the coming of San Francisco and his blessing. It was not too late— not if it happened within the year. The least one would still be a burrito, ungalled, with swiftness to his hoofs and lightness to his heart. A blessing from San Francisco within the year would save him from that which had already overtaken him—the burden cloth, the great loads, the constant toiling.

Paco's feet made short work of climbing the hill to his home. They hopped up the steep incline like Mexican jumping beans—two of them. Their very antics made Paco laugh until he had to stop for breath. "No days to come after will be as bad as this one, or as long as this one, or as troublesome," he promised himself. And then he shouted to the rooster on the ridge pole of the hut: "Olé, Galleto, I come!"

He swung in through the bamboo gate. There against the old banana tree stood his father. But what made him look as he did? He was much of the same color as the long hanging leaves, a kind of pale green, very unhealthy-looking. Paco approached him with eagerness and as one man may approach another. His thumbs were digging themselves into the knot where his shirt-ends were tied. "Papá! Papá chico! I work now for Manuel, the sandal-maker. He gave me the compliment today of being a good apprentice in the first day of making. Where is Chiquitico?"

Even while he was talking his eyes had told him the unbelievable truth, that there were but two burros in the enclosure, cropping the weeds along the barranca. And neither of them was the least one. Two burros; no more, no less. "He is, perhaps, down the barranca. I will look." Paco said this hopefully.

"Thou wilt not look!" commanded Vicente.

"Perhaps I cannot count," suggested Paco. "I say, with the help of my fingers, one—two, just that: one—two. But of a truth there may be three burros, yonder."

"There are two." Vicente said it with great firmness.

"Then where—papacito—where is Chiquitico!" This time Paco wailed the words like a lamentation.

A hush had fallen on all things. The ups-and-downs, all creatures, even earth and sky appeared to be holding their breath. Rosa came to the doorway to see what had put so unusual a silence upon everything.

It was with a kind of patient anger that Vicente spoke: "Basta! What is the matter with all of you? You look at me as if I were a stranger. Rosa—I ask thee—am I not still thy husband? Good! José-Ana-Claudio-Paco-Felipe-Juanita-Rafael, I ask you—am I not still your father? Good! Then talk to me no more about that rascal of a burrito. He is gone. He will never return. If anyone now asks you how many burros has Vicente Rabell you will answer 'Two.' Two! Dost thou understand, Paco?"

"I understand. Two."

He watched his father go to the table under the thatch, sit down and wait for Rosa to bring out the evening meal. When she called them to table, Paco could not remove his back from the papaya trunk which held him up. Eat! His stomach revolted at the thought of putting anything more into it than the misery it already held. What terrible thing had happened to the least one? Was it witchcraft? Were the stories that the charcoal burners told over the pits true? Twice he moistened his lips before he could ask of Vicente: "Papá, didst thou by any chance borrow fire from a strange woman today?"

Vicente put down his knife and stared at his son in wonder. "Hast thou taken a sunstroke to ask such foolishness? Why should I borrow fire, with good matches always on me?"

Of course. No one longer borrowed fire, not since the good matches found their way into the poorest of pockets. He was a bobo, a foolish one, to ask it. Paco's eyes went back to the two burros, the small and the little ones. Could they tell him what had happened to the least one? Had they seen? "Aí de mi!" His wail of anguish went up like smoke, skywards. His eyes followed. Overhead three zopilotes skimmed the air, circled, and glided down over the village. Could one of them be

the least one? And would he ever know? Would he ever eat tamales and chile, beans and tortillas again with appetite? He doubted it. For him the end of the world had come. For centuries his people had said that some day Popocatepetl would vomit and the world would be destroyed. For him—he didn't care how soon it happened.

THE PHOTOGRAPHER BEGINS TO
GROW RICH

THROUGH the days that followed, Paco went about on feet heavier than nothing. Sharply he scanned every pack train, counting them, making sure that the most beautiful burro in all of Mexico, in the Atlantic and Pacific Oceans, in the United States, in the family of Vicente Rabell, was not among them. After work he scoured the countryside, making sure no farmer had acquired a new gray-and-white burrito. But nowhere did he find Chiquitico. The earth might have swallowed him. Or a witch had changed him into a gray zopilote. There were plenty of those overhead.

Every night Paco returned to the hut, his heart a pit of blackness, even like the charcoal pits. Food—he could not eat it. The good atole —he could not drink it. And when he looked up at the dark dome of the sky and saw the stars he could have cried out in bitter pain. What use now was it for the fastenings of the Holy Ones to give way? Who cared if the good San Francisco came to earth to bless his creatures? The least one would not be there to be blessed.

Vicente watched his middle-born while a black fear settled about his own heart. He loved them all, the ups-and-downs; but he was of the secret opinion that Paco was the smartest, the most likely to get on. What now if the boy's life should wither away because of a curse and a worthless burro! Could God be about to punish him that way for his wickedness? It was not to be believed. And yet, no longer was there the happiness, the contentment that had always dwelt among them. Laughter came seldom. Something altogether troubling had come over the family of Vicente Rabell and left them all of a kind of woodenness, so Vicente thought.

A week went heavily by. At the end of it, Paco, returning from the fábrica, found an unexpected crowd gathered in the Zócalo. Tourists and boot-cleaners, postcard venders, idlers, and shopkeepers were jostling one another under the big ahuehuete tree in the exact spot where Pedro Villa usually stood, waiting for trade. Pedro was one of the village photographers. Juan Cuerva was the other. Between the two existed hot rivalry, made hotter because Juan had a dappled wooden mount for his patrons, and Pedro had none.

All in the village had heard Pedro say, jerking his thumb toward Juan Cuerva: "If I had a mount, even as that one, I would not be a poor man. I would marry my Consuela on Easter Monday. But all want their pictures taken astride a beast—even a wooden one. What good does it do me to be the artist—to know how to make all men look the caballero, and all women pretty!"

Paco had reached the last outposts and was about to get to his feet when something caught his eye, something fixed to a wooden board on wheels. Four slender gray-and-white legs!

Paco, remaining crouched like el soltero, the frog, on his belly, desired above all things not to be noticed. His heart was in his throat, trying to strangle him. What he saw was absurd, impossible, but there it was.

In the open spot, taking up all the room that Pedro, his camera, his bucket, and his bottles did not occupy, was the least one. There was the

same white marking like an outspread hand between the eyes; there was the same nick in the tip of one ear; there was the same white fetlock on one hind leg, a gray one on the other. It was a burro of the same littleness and perfect proportions, of the same gray-and-whiteness as Chiquitico. But what a Chiquitico!

There he stood, immovable, nailed to a board that ran on wheels. He was as wooden as the board. His eyes stared; his ears were without delicious twitchings; his tail hung heavily behind like the clapper on a bell. Upon his back was a serape, and over that a saddle. In his mouth was a bridle, studded with brass, and sitting in the saddle, sombrero on his head, a neckerchief about his throat, a lariat in his hand, sat Ignacio, son of the silversmith—a boy who gave himself abominable airs and whom Paco detested.

It was so sickening, so terrible. It was witchcraft. Otherwise how could a live, flesh-and-blood burro be turned to wood? The old Indian tales the charcoal burners told were true. Whatever had happened it was evil.

As Paco had crawled in, so did he crawl out. Free of the crowd, he got to his legs and ran as if the devil himself were after him. That night he did not touch the fresh-made tortillas, the beans, or the rice. He did not dare ask Vicente about the new thing in the Zócalo. He had no longer heart for anything, and suddenly he pushed away his still filled plate and bolted from the table.

He made for the barranca, the bottom of it. There he found el soltero sitting fat and well fed, catching the last beams of the sun on his green back. Paco threw himself down on the dry gravel of the bed. Now that he had no longer a talking-mate he would take the frog, the best that was left.

"Rana," he said in a smothered voice, "listen!" And then he could not say it; he could not put into words the dreadful thing that had happened. When he could use words he used them raggedly: "It looks like witches' work—but—but—the papá knows. It is what turned him green—that day—that day that only two burros came home. What am I to do! Look at what stands in the Zócalo? Every day to see it! I tell you it is no good to ask the papá anything. What happened has gone down so far inside of him it will never come up."

El soltero closed his eyes. He had gone to sleep. It was probable he had heard nothing of what Paco with such difficulty had told him. Puf! What was the use of talking to a frog? They were stupid; they understood nothing. And yet the boy waited and waited. The bachelor might make some answer—blow a bubble or flick an eye. But he kept on doing nothing until Paco, in disgust, touched him quickly with a stick. Whereupon el soltero sprang, making a long leap across the barranca, disappearing into the fastness of many great rocks.

Paco buried his head in his arms and burst into a downpour of tears, smarting, galling tears that eased the aching in his heart. Aí—how should he meet and march with the endless procession of days ahead? How should he stand the aloneness that was now his!

Rosa, looking for him, heard his wailing. She stood on the bank above, Rafael in her arms. Her voice was not ungentle, neither was it greatly concerned. "Thou hast nothing about which to cry. Thy papá is not dead. I am not dead. There are none of us about to die. Get up and find the pig, the one with brown patches. He has been gone since mid-day."

Paco found the pig. It was good to have something to do. With a willow switch he guided him back to the yard. There Claudio challenged him to a game of bottle-tops. It is a game all Mexican boys play. It begins by collecting the bottle-tops from the hotels, from the cafés. When one has his pockets full, he challenges another with full pockets. The game goes on until all the bottle-tops change pockets and the winner has two full. Paco won, and went off to idle in the yard, to watch from the gate who might be passing up or down the road.

Vicente joined him and spoke: "Manuel says thou art a good apprentice indeed. It is even possible that after seven years thou mayest be a good sandal-maker. I would not be surprised if one day thou shouldst make sandals for the Presidente."

"A sandal-maker makes much money, yes?"

"Truly. One can get rich that way."

"Then in seven years I will have money to buy whatever I want, yes?"

"Thou couldst not buy the City of Mexico, nor the world."

"Who would want them? But I could buy a burro, papá?"

"What wouldst thou want with a burro, and thou a sandal-maker? An automobile, now, that would be something."

"I would not want an automobile. I would want only a burro. If I am to be a sandal-maker, I buy what I want."

Paco was thinking that it was not for nothing he was standing the cooped-up hours in the fábrica, the soaking of hides in the vats and the unspeakable stench of them, to have no eyes free to watch the sun cross the heavens, to see nothing of the waxing and waning day, to miss the shadows of the clouds and the zopilotes' wings moving, always moving across the high hills. To miss all this in these glorious days of being very young one must have much to make up for it afterwards.

Meanwhile Vicente was thinking that here was a son of great spirit.

It would take much to break it. Here was one who would not be lazy, who would have the mind to make for himself a goal worth a struggle. Here was a man in the making. One day he might make the name of Rabell a great one. The Presidente had been such a boy.

Paco broke that thinking. "But I do not want any burro I can buy, papá. I want one special burro." He waited there for what Vicente might ask.

Being shrewd, Vicente asked nothing.

Paco's voice took on a bravery that surprised himself. "Papá chico, is it not possible some day, not too soon, perhaps, but before I am too old to be happy again, is it not possible that the least one will come back to us?"

"That good-for-nothing! He will never come. He is gone forever. How many times must I say it!"

"But, papá, if he should come, that good-for-nothing burrito, could he be mine?"

As bravery grew on Paco's tongue, impatience grew on Vicente's. "Qué estúpido! Thou art a bobo to keep asking. I tell thee he will never..."

"But should he? Papacito, make me some kind of an answer and I will keep quiet."

Vicente shrugged his shoulders. "Well then, Señor Sandal-Maker, should he come he shall be wholly thine."

Paco breathed exquisite hope down the length of him. Here was something, a promise. And for tonight, tomorrow, all the tomorrows, he would have a kind of ownership in the least one, no matter where he stood, no matter of what he was made. Secretly he could say to himself at any hour of the day, or night if he were awake, Chiquitico is wholly mine; the papá has said so. But this did not satisfy him. He must have the promise sworn on something holy. "Papá, it would make my stomach more content if thou wouldst promise it upon my name saint."

A look of something akin to amazement crossed Vicente's face. He stooped and looked curiously into the face of the boy. He laid a firm and promising hand upon Paco's shoulder. "The least one shall be thine, I swear it on the name of the saint who loveth all creatures, the good San Francisco."

Long after the others were asleep inside the jacal Paco stayed awake that he might tell the Holy Mother about this momentous promise. Not a breath of wind stirred through the bamboos; the flame of the fat little candle rose without a flicker, straight heavenwards. Making sure that no ear other than the Holy Mother's was awake to listen, Paco knelt on his cane-leaves in the corner and began by clasping his hands very tight. But as his supplications rose, he was forced to unclasp them that he might make gestures to give strength to his words.

"Thou wilt tell him, Madre mía, the promise made by papá, a certain carrier by the name of Vicente Rabell, and a truly good man. It is possible that San Francisco passes the Throne of Heaven every night and that Thou knowest him well. But in case he is somewhat of a stranger, he is the small brown brother in sandaled feet, a rope about his middle, and the halo somewhat crooked and not too well burnished. He always carries a lamb in his arms, too. Thou wilt likely hear it bleating as he comes.

"Santa María, it is for this reason that I supplicate Thee. Por favor, Thou wilt tell him of the burrito, the one of a gray-and-whiteness, and most to be desired of all burritos, that has been turned into wood not many days now. Tell the Saint that he is to be mine if ever he comes back to flesh-and-bloodness. And if San Francisco could get himself unfastened from the sky and drop down to earth, beg him to drop on this village. His blessing on the burrito would make all right again. Tell him that, por favor, Blessed Mother."

There was much more, said very confidentially, as one speaks to another one can trust and knows will understand. Sticks scratched in Paco's eyes until he closed them for a little longer each time, until the figure of the Blessed Mother blurred into nothingness. He mumbled timidly: "Thou mightest smile to show Thou hast understood, or rustle Thy mantle . . ."

Paco could never be sure when his eyelids had closed, when he had crumpled down on the cane-leaves. He could never be sure whether the Blessed Mother had smiled or not. But he was certain that she had understood. This was in his mind the moment that everything had become nothing and nothing had become next morning.

That noontime he offered his services to Pedro to mind the camera and all else during the hour for comida. He promised solemnly not to take an eye off anything. The photographer hesitated, casting a doubtful look in the direction of his rival. "That Juan Cuerva"—he did not lower his voice—"he would give his back teeth to have what I have. What is a horse now, what good to him, when I have the only burro in all of Mexico upon which to mount my patrons! It is now I who get the trade. I tell thee thou must watch that hombre with the eye of a zopilote."

Paco agreed. And from that day when Pedro went home for his dinner he was free to whisper his ownership into the stiff, untwitching ears of the least one. "Thou art wholly mine. Let the man who wheels thee think what he pleases. I have spoken to the Blessed Mother, who will speak to our saint. Thou wilt see; some day it will happen and thou shalt be free of thy board and wheels and I of the vats and the goat-hides."

Days became weeks by the simple multiple of seven; and every day there was something new to tell the least one. Secret after secret was poured into his unattending ears. Every day Paco gathered fresh dreams of the things that they would do, the places they would go when the miracle should come to pass. And between the whisperings he drummed up much trade for Pedro. Let a tourist, a stranger come within earshot of the burrito and Paco was on his feet, shouting his praises. "Look! It is a great honor to be taken with the only real photographer's burro in the world. Is he not beautiful? Is he not animated? And it costs no more than a common picture taken on a horse."

But all days were not alike. There were days when Paco's heart drifted so downwards that, as he said, he walked on it. On those days everything about the fábrica sickened him: the parrot on his perch outside scoffed at him. The call of forests, of the hillsides and the valleys seemed to smother him. At the noon hour when he let his hands move over the least one, there was conveyed to him such a hardness, such an unyielding woodenness, that he doubted if even the blessing of San Francisco could perform a miracle.

So his heart went up and his heart went down, and on the good days he never failed to whisper to the least one: "Forget not the good San Francisco, ever. Some day we will be kicking our heels together on the hills once more. We will become merchants, carrying small things that women need into the little far-off villages. Ohu! It will be magnificent, but first there must be money. Money to buy light baskets for thy back; money to buy those woman-things to sell; money to share with the papá, that he will not feel too badly that the third burro is no longer his." So did Paco wind his imagination like a moist strand of silk over and over in his mind. And there it was to unwind whenever he had time for delicious fancies.

But this did not make him like the work of an apprentice any better. He might be a good one but he loathed everything that took place within the shop. Why should anyone wear sandals when the warm earth felt life-giving under one's feet? Where did the work of a sandal-maker get one? On the hillsides were goat-paths to lead one to enchanting places; but this soaking and beating and drying and cutting up what once had been goat—it left one still imprisoned. And the next day one did the same things all over again. Puf—what a life!

To break up the days and bring something new into them, Paco became more than an apprentice to Manuel Juárez. Having that watchful eye for business with which most Mexican boys are born, he advertised sandals on his way to and from the shop. He enticed customers to follow him inside. He would lead them up to the door with a magnificent flourish and speak loudly and distinctly those words of English he had picked up from the tourists in the Zócalo: "Come een. Veree good. Veree cheap. You like? Scram!"

Now the sandal-maker was a just man. He watched Paco. First he only praised his success and loyalty to a patrón; then, as more customers came and bought because of his beguiling ways, Manuel considered this was not the work the boy was bound for, that he was entitled to something more than an apprentice's training. So he set aside a quinto, a five-penny piece, for everyone who bought because of Paco. These he gave to him at the end of the day.

Paco tied the coins in the tail of his lavender shirt. On handsprings he covered the length of the street to the Zócalo. There he must show his wealth to Pedro, untying the knot in his shirt, displaying the coins in his palm. "Hombre, look, all because I speak English very well and bring business to the patrón. It is the beginning of my fortune. Our fortune." He laid a hand over the saddle of the least one's back.

Now Pedro, likewise, was a just man. This gave him thought. Had not the boy brought him business as well? Was it not almost a daily occurrence that when he returned from eating at the noon hour that the boy had a customer, sometimes two, waiting for him? He could afford to be generous even as the sandal-maker, although not quite so generous. He looked again at the coins. "So—the sandal-maker can pay for honest service. Well—so can Pedro Villa. Not so much, perhaps, but something. There shall be a penny for every customer thou wheedlest. Está contento?"

Was he contented! Paco performed gymnastics in the park. Never had he dreamed of such a chance to acquire riches like these. "I shall now have two fortunes," he shouted.

That night he put the first coins down the neck of a dry gourd and hid it in the bottom of the barranca, making el soltero the guardian of it. "Rana—listen! Thou must tell no one. It will grow like the seed in the ground, this fortune, and some day it will be more enormous than nothing."

He was thinking very well of himself when he joined the family for supper. It had been a good day of carrying for Vicente; the family were eating well. There was mole as well as the rice and beans with chile. Paco ate until his small belly was full and well rounded, until he could pat it with the contentment he had not known since the least one had not come home. He said to Vicente, Rosa, and the ups-and-downs in the voice of one who has struggled hard and conquered all: "I think it will not be too many years, not more than fifty, before the papá will not have to work so hard and I shall be a man of fortune."

The magnificence of these words sent him spry-legged up one of the goat-paths, disappearing behind a clump of high organ cacti, leaving his family gazing after him with a dumbness and a popeyedness not unlike that of el soltero.

All I have told you happened during the first weeks of the year. Carnival time came. It began in February and it would end with the beginning of the Holy Season. As there had come many tourists to Mexico that winter there was more money than usual for everyone to spend, and everyone was in high good humor. The Carnival-makers brought their tents and set them up around the Zócalo. Under the big

ahuehuete tree was erected with much care and excitement Los Caballitos—The Little Horses—or as the American children would call
them, the Merry-Go-Round.

Every day music came out of a tin box; the horses whirled and every
rider had a sword strapped to his saddle. This was to draw, to make
thrusts at the iron rings as one whirled by, in the expectation of getting
the one gold ring in the lot. Whoever presented the gold ring to the
patrón of Los Caballitos received a prize.

Every boy or girl who had a quinto rode once and talked about it all
the rest of the year. Some, like Ignacio, the son of the silversmith, rode
every day. Paco watched him, and his fingers itched to punch him once,
hard, as he got off his horse. Paco watched with much satisfaction to
see would he get the gold ring. But he never did; that was something.
Paco's fingers itched further. Never did he come to the Zócalo with one
of Manuel's quintos tied up in the tail of his lavender shirt that he was
not almost overcome with the desire to ride Los Caballitos. Never had
he whirled to the music of the tin box; never had he had a sword to
brandish and thrust. And might not he get a prize worth far more
than the quinto paid for the ride?

At these times, while he watched others whirl, especially when Ignacio was calling all attention to his horse and his sword, a strange and
very loud voice spoke within Paco and urged him most abominably to
pay out his quinto and ride with the rest. What was money for but to
spend? And the sensation—think of that! Where else would he ever
gain so much heart-beating pleasure? Every day the voice grew louder,
more insistent, until Paco almost believed a rascal of a boy, more wild
and stronger than himself, had taken up living-quarters within him.

Enchiladas

STATE STREET METHODIST CHURCH LIBRARY
BRISTOL, VIRGINIA

He got to shouting back at him so that if the music from the tin box had not been very loud and overpowering the onlookers would have thought Paco quite crazy. But it was the only way to get the rascal in hand, to shout at the top of his voice: "Abominations! I have not time for such idleness. I am now a man of business. It takes a long time to earn five pennies. They are not to be thrown away for a moment of foolishness."

Before the rascal could get in another word, Paco would march himself off, to remove himself from temptation, to carry his quinto up the hill and drop it with deep satisfaction into the gourd, replacing that in el soltero's keeping; that was victory, and victory had its glorious moment.

But Los Caballitos was not all that tempted Paco. Stands with bright awnings, red and green, rose and blue, yellow and purple, opened up like amaryllis under the Carnival sun. The air became laden with odors of buñuelos, enchiladas, tamales, coffee being freshly roasted over the charcoal braziers on the street corners; ripe, fragrant pineapples, sliced on platters, ready to eat; glass jars filled with iced drinks. A boy could not sit in the Zócalo five minutes and not have his nostrils twitched by these tantalizing smells. Paco would pin his mind hard to the business of getting customers for Pedro, but the rascal within him could always drown out his calling.

"Thou hast many times five pennies. Smell the good smells. Thou art empty as a dried gourd. This moment thou couldst eat up the whole Zócalo and still have room for thy mother's supper. Well—why wait? Try the enchiladas; try one enchilada."

More than once in these moments of diabolical temptation Paco had to grip hard to the solid frame of the least one to remind himself in quick succession of many things: the need of much more money than he yet had, the coming and blessing of San Francisco—any day—any hour, the promises he had made Chiquitico that they would again be kicking heels in free, far-off places. All this was anchorage for Paco, and he would weather through that worst and return home with his pennies unspent. Ohu—it was a good feeling, once over with.

Paco thanked his guiding star when Carnival was over, when the sober abstinence of the Holy Season began. The rascal left him, and no more did he hear his voice. He shook all pennies and quintos out of the gourd one star-filled night and counted them. It was incredible but it was true! He had altogether, counting five to every quinto, more than fifty pennies. They lay there in his hand; he could hold them, feel them, know them for his own. If he had eaten of the stuff in the Zócalo where would they have been now!

On two days of every week, Rosa carried the family clothes to the estanque, on the street above the Zócalo, where the stream from the mountains was piped down in thick lead pipes, to run in turn through earthen ones that emptied into the stone washing-place. Slanting stones were placed in even rows along one side, and it was on these that the clothes were soaped and rubbed clean, later to be rinsed and wrung out, to go wet into the baskets. The ups helped Rosa to fetch the washing to and from the estanque, and helped her again to hang the wet clothes in the yard to dry. The next day she made them smooth with flat, heated stones. Rosa took a bursting pride in having Vicente and the older boys go clean every day when they went to work, and on Sundays to have the whole family clean.

Every Sunday morning, Rosa would call: "José-Ana-Claudio-Paco-Felipe-Juanita-Rafael-get-ready-for-mass." That meant each in turn, except Rafael, would carry the one cake of soap down to the pool at the bottom of the barranca to wash their heads, their hands, their necks, usually their ears, and sometimes behind their ears. Then they would wash their feet, always their feet. Each in turn would come up, careful not to spatter dust on the altogether-cleanness. Each would change with no little excitement into the clean splendor, laid out to avoid mussing, on the matrimonio. Always for Vicente and the boys there were white cotton pants and shirts of solid colors: pink, orange, blue, lavender were the favorites. Paco always saw to it that he was one of the first to wash so that he could have a lavender shirt. He enjoyed mass and all the rest of the week far more if he did not have to wear one of another color. No family in all the village owned more splendor in the matter of shirts. All the boys and Vicente slicked down their wet hair with a little oil and smoothed and smoothed with the palms of both hands until their heads glistened like the sleek breasts of young crows.

Rosa and the girls had variegated cotton dresses and dark blue rebosas. The rebosas they wore over their heads to protect them from the sun; they wore them to cover their heads at mass; they wore them wrapped close about their slim bodies to keep them warm in the cool evenings, and when there was a baby like Rafael, or a heavy load to carry, they slung these in the rebosas under their arms. There was a family comb, lacking two teeth, and every Sunday morning Rosa combed her hair and the hair of all the little girls and braided it in two long braids to each head. Seldom on week days was the hair combed, but on Sundays, yes, and with tight braiding it lasted well through the

next six days. To have a comb and a cake of soap, that was something.

When all were ready they formed a procession, one by one, going down the hill to the cathedral. Vicente and the boys led, Rosa with Rafael slung in her rebosa followed, and the little girls came after her. So gay a pattern of print dresses and colored shirts they made that they looked like a Mexican garden on the march.

Behind them they left the turkey, dusting himself, the pigeons hunting for seeds, the hens scratching, the pigs rooting in every direction, the goats wandering off for fodder, and Chico and Chiquita lying under the shade of the jacaranda tree. They knew, these two, that this was the day which the good God had set aside that His lowliest creatures might rest. So flat and still they lay that they might well have been shadows, cast there by the sun.

The cock only remains to be told about. He considered that Sunday belonged to him. He strutted until all had passed through the bamboo gate. Then he flew to the ridge pole of the hut where he made himself patrón over all Vicente's possessions. Whenever a passer-by went up or down the road he flapped his wings and crowed: "Kikiriki—kikiriki!" telling the world that all this belonged to him.

On the last Sunday of Carnival, Pedro Villa, the photographer, had felt himself to be so rich that he had broken no less than twenty colored and perfumed eggs over the head of his novia, Consuela, as they passed each other in the long paseo. The band played splendid American tunes. The boys moved one way on the outside circle of the Zócalo; the girls, arms linked, moved in the opposite direction so that girls and boys were always meeting. This was their one chance of courting: to exchange adoring words, to cast admiring glances, to give a token. But only at Carnival time were the colored eggs full of water, perfume, or confetti bought and broken by the young men upon the girls of their choice. No matter how uncomfortable this deluge might be, it was a sign of admiration, especially the perfumed eggs. Always it had to be received with smiles and giggles. The girl upon whom the most eggs had been broken became the belle of the Carnival. On this year Consuela was the belle.

All through the last evening, Paco sat next to one of the fat Indian women who had eggs to sell. He knew that probably for a year she had been saving those eggs, blowing out the contents to use for cooking, dyeing the shells all colors, filling their emptiness with something, and sealing the holes with gummed paper. If it was a gay Carnival, she would sell a hundred or more. That was good business.

Sitting there, thinking, Paco had an idea. When he became a merchant of the road, with the least one to carry the basket, confetti and perfume and dye would be among the things to carry to the small, far-off villages. In such a one, he knew, the whole village collected eggs for one to color and sell. He sat, savoring his thoughts, swinging his brown feet, watching with gusto every glance exchanged, every gesture. He counted the eggs Pedro broke, and when the number passed twenty he ran to Vicente and Rosa, who were watching at the other side of the Zócalo, and shouted: "That Pedro and that Consuela, they will be married at Easter. You will see. He is cracking eggs on her as if they cost nothing."

Paco went back to his seat beside the egg-basket. It was amusing to watch, but money was for more important things. He saw his prophecy come true before his eyes. He marked Pedro's growing excitement with every turn of the paseo. The man was shouting his laughter and all were shouting with him. At last, as he passed Consuela, he pulled her out of the circle; he brought her before the place where her family was seated; he shouted in a voice for all the world to hear: "We marry on the Monday of Easter. Tell the mamá and papá, the sisters and brothers, the aunts and uncles and the cousins, that everyone may know and come."

And Paco in delight shouted as loudly as Pedro: "They have heard. They will come. There is no need to tell."

THE GOOD SAN FRANCISCO GETS
NEW SANDALS

On the morning of Easter Monday, Paco dressed early and went down to the Zócalo long before he would be expected for vat-stirring at the sandal-maker's. He wished to speak to Pedro. He could guess the photographer's intentions: to catch all the wedding crowd before the wedding and, afterwards, to take many pictures and make much money. To be a bridegroom in no way interfered with being a man of business. Already he had offered Paco a quinto to mind everything while the ceremony was being performed. But Paco had an idea beyond that. That was why he arrived early.

Pedro was already there, arranging everything for a good day. Paco pulled his sleeve many times before he could get his attention. "Listen, hombre, when the time comes, we will carry the pail and the camera into Doña Berta's cantina and leave them there. Then I will pull the burrito to the cathedral so that we may both see thee married."

Pedro was shocked. "We will do nothing of the sort. Is the holy church a place to pasture burros? Thou art a bobo to think of such a thing. And the village would talk about it for a year—to see a wooden burro follow me to the high altar!"

But Paco was not to be discouraged. He gathered up his reasons; he had been collecting them for days. Was it not because of the burrito that Pedro had become rich? Would there be any wedding this day if,

59

in some mysterious way unknown to himself or to anyone else, the burrito had not come into his possession? And were there not already creatures of wood and creatures of wax inside the cathedral? San José had a burrito, not so beautiful but still not unlike this one. San Francisco had his wooden lamb. And besides there were doves, and a little dog. It was Pedro who was the bobo. Surely...

In great annoyance the photographer shook off the hand that was holding him. He was in fear that in spite of all his resolutions this bleating boy would have his way with him. "I tell thee no! I tell thee a three-times no! It is one thing for the saints to bring in wooden creatures if they wish, but not for me. That would be a sacrilege. Remember that every creature inside has been blessed."

Paco drew in his breath and let it out with great silence. Pedro must not know that the reasons spoken were nothing compared to that one reason he had left unsaid, this very matter of blessing. If he could get the least one inside the cathedral once, the blessing might happen! Cautiously he felt for words: "But, hombre, it would not be a bad thing for thee—thy business—if the burrito here were taken inside with the creatures who have been blessed. Maybe the blessing is catching, like fleas and the scarlet fever."

"Bah! Give over thy talking. What does it matter to me whether he be blessed or not? I think thou hast a touch of sun; thou art altogether crazy. Come back at the hour and earn the quinto by doing as thou hast been told."

To have one's great idea smashed into gravel! Aí—his mouth tasted of it, his stomach was full of it. Now what to do? To soak hides, to smell them, to give attention to what the older apprentices did and how they did it. It was all of a nothingness. In a kind of despair he went down the street to Manuel's shop.

At the wedding hour, from the raised level of the Zócalo, Paco could watch the crowd going into the cathedral. Pedro had left to go home and put on his new wedding finery, a dark suit, a red-and-purple tie, a hat to carry. Without permission, Paco did not dare enter the cathedral, but with the crowd inside he dared a little more than he had been told to do. He carried the camera and pail and gave them into Doña Berta's charge. Then he ran quickly back and dragged the least one across the street and through the iron gates that set the cathedral apart from the village square. Between the gates and the cathedral stretched a large, pleasant garden. A firm-packed, broad path led to the main door. A bougainvillaea vine of giant height and magnificence filled nearly one side of the garden. In the shade of this he and the least one could stand and watch all coming out.

Over the great door was set in the stone arch a bas-relief. Paco had never looked carefully at it, had never been interested in what it pictured. All churches had something over their main doorways. But now he had to stand a long time with nothing to do but look. Time had dimmed the outline of the figures; lichens had grown in patches over them, but his eyes began to pick out details here and there. He picked out the heads of an ox, a deer, a dog, a goat, a wolf, a bear, and a burro. These heads were set in curlicues and garlands of stone. Below, in the archway, he made out a kneeling figure with more animals grouped about it. These he could not trace clearly, but something in the flowing robes of the figure, the broken halo about its head, made him wonder. Could this be an outside San Francisco? The feet looked sandaled; the broken line of the waist looked like a twisted rope. Was this a stone brother to the figure inside?

Paco was amazed; he was delighted. He thrust his hands under the burrito's nose and tried to tilt it upwards. "Chiquitico, it is possible that is thy saint and mine. I think he is all the time blessing those creatures about him. Look at the head the third from this end. It is a burro as plain as thou art one. Thou rememberest long ago, the night of many stars, how I talked to thee about the Holy Ones dropping from the sky. I don't know what good it would do, but it might keep him thinking about it, that San Francisco, if we lighted a candle here in the doorway. That would not be a bad way to spend a penny or two. Perhaps he does not like it that we put all in the gourd and remember him not at all. We will change that, yes?"

That was the beginning of the mystery of the lighted candle about which Padre Anselmo spoke often and about which Paco said nothing. The padre said no one was seen placing it there; it was done in the depths of the night and found burning always in the morning. Always the padre carried it inside the church and let it burn out its life before the shrine of San Francisco. But he wondered much why the candle was put always in the doorway, under the stone saint, almost obliterated by time.

The spring rains came. They filled the barranca with a swift, foaming torrent. Paco rescued the gourd from the rocks in the nick of time and hid it under the earth, at the roots of the banana tree, where it was easy to dig. Through the spring his mind dwelt much on miracles, the possibility of them, the ease with which they might be performed.

He remembered only one miracle ever happening in the village and that was a hundred years ago, when a little girl named Rosario had gone into the cathedral on a cold night to pray. She had looked up at the Gentle Jesus on the cross, so naked, so cold, and in pity had taken her rebosa and wrapped it about Him. The next day—there it was—turned to cloth of gold for all to see. Now if one miracle could take

place in the village, two could. After a hundred years it was time another was performed there.

El soltero, the fat frog, had left the barranca on the first drop of the rains and had gone on his spring courting. Paco heard him rumbling his love-song as he went. When the waters had thinned out to a shallow trickle he would be back again. Then, Paco knew, he could return the gourd with safety to the rocks. In the days of old, feathered serpents were supposed to guard treasure in Mexico, but a fat green frog was not so bad as a guardian.

Summer comes gently in Mexico. She is like a kind grandmother who has little to do and can gather her grandchildren into her lap and sing them into drowsy contentment. She has a new and a different song for every hour of the day and night. She can sing away all hunger and all cold. She stretches forth her hands and blesses all new-born creatures, all new-planted things. The rains that covered the earth before her coming, the frosts that will follow after her—these are all forgotten. Her hair is a pale yellow, the color of the silk on the ripening maize. She wears the sky upon it and crosses it over her breast like a rebosa. Some of her songs have names. There is the song of the falling dew, the song of the breaking day, the song of the flight of birds, the song of the noonday siesta, the song for labor, and the song for pleasure. She is a good grandmother, summer.

Vicente had plowed his small patch of fertile ground with the slackening of the rains. He had used the strong, seasoned root of a tree for a plow, with the small one to drag it. He had planted maize, squash, peppers, beans, onions. There was plenty to eat. Vicente did not have to work every day. Had there been three burros instead of two at rest outside the jacal during the hottest days, to feel the cool winds at night suck down from the mountains, to listen to the soft, persuading call of the tórtola—the wood-dove—ohu, all would have been contentment in the family of Vicente Rabell.

Every other week—Paco notched them on the trunk of the papaya—he lighted his candle in the doorway of the cathedral, secretly, at dead of night. And one day as he watched an apprentice gather up the scraps of leather and throw them out he had an inspiration—enormous! magnificent! He had noticed as he had prayed before the small figure of the inside San Francisco that the sandals on his feet looked old and badly worn. If he could learn enough to make him a new pair! That would be something to draw his attention. And did not all Holy Ones repay benefits showered upon them—especially when offered with a loving heart?

After that Paco gathered the cast-off scraps of leather. Every spare moment through the day he stood, silent, beside the third-year apprentices and watched them mark the soles, fasten the strips of leather, and weave them. The sandal-maker noticed and railed him over his hoarding and his eagerness to learn. "Thou wilt learn in a year what it takes most apprentices three to learn, yes? And what dost thou intend doing with the scraps? Art thou to be a sandal-maker for children or for dolls?"

Paco went on about his business of cleaning up and answered: "It is my secret. I may be making sandals for the burros—or it may be for the hidden people. There are some things best not spoken of."

"He has wisdom—that one," laughed the patrón.

The men were amused. They got into the habit of letting Paco help them wax their threads, hand them the strips of leather, pull them into place. They showed him how a good workman used his awl. And be-

tween suppertime and dark Paco would take his scraps down, into the barranca, safe from the curious eyes of the ups-and-downs, and practice with his hands what he had seen with his eyes.

At first it was hopeless. He was clumsy, he could make nothing go right. Then the trick of it began to come; his fingers stopped going their clumsy ways and obeyed his direction. When that moment came he shouted exultantly to the frog: "Rana—the thumb now knows its business! The fingers listen to what I tell them. Tomorrow night we begin a small pair of sandals for a Holy One."

All the colors of the rainbow went into those sandals for San Francisco. Never had a saint possessed such splendid footwear. Ohu, but it would look beautiful with the saint's brown robe! Often after the day's work Paco would enter the cathedral, kneel before the niche that held San Francisco, and, making his lips move as if in prayer, give his whole attention to the exact size and shape of the Holy One's foot. That is how it came to pass that on the morning early, following that night on which the sandals were finished, Paco was able to take off the old ones and put on the new, quickly, before any saw him. They fitted to a perfection that made his heart sing, and he went back, through the doorway, making his reverences impartially to both San Franciscos—the one inside, the one out: "Sandals for thee—candles for thee! Prayers and offerings for both. Remember that!"

Autumn took summer's place. There were redder sunrises, more purple and golden sunsets than summer could give. Such a glory of colors made even a small Mexican boy catch at his breath. "I think the Holy Ones are making a procession in the sky. It is the color of their vestments—the light from their candles—the spattering from their church windows that light up the heavens."

All the family of Vicente were making ready for the winter. Sacks of maize, shelled and hanging from the poles in the lean-to, drying, peppers strung for chile, beans drying in their pods, and coffee-beans, in pans out in the sun, making ready for roasting. When the green shells were dry enough Rosa would call: "Come-José-Ana-Claudio-Paco-Felipe-Juanita-Rafael-make-the-hands-to-fly!"

It was a good feeling, this of harvest, and it went on and on, a little to do every day while the days shortened and the weather ripened everything. Every day at least one of the hens laid a fat brown egg. A good year was counting its tenth month.

The very first Sunday in October an amazing thing happened at
mass. After the sermon—after all had been blessed—the padre had
made a most astonishing announcement. Every word of it ding-donged
its way into Paco's brain like a clamoring bell. The padre had said:
"My children, I have good news for you. It is now many years since we
have kept the Day of San Francisco. It is many years since you have
been allowed to bring any living creature to the gardens of the cathedral that it might be blessed. But through long intercession our Presidente has at last come to realize what this fiesta means to the people of
this village. Therefore, upon Tuesday next, permission has been
granted to celebrate the day. You may bring what living creature you
will at the hour of oraciones."

Paco's heart stopped beating altogether, started again, stopped, and
then it seemed it would never go. The Day of San Francisco—two days
off—the creatures to be blessed again. All creatures! "You may bring
what you will"—the padre had said it; he had said nothing against
bringing a wooden creature. Or had he? Paco thought back to the beginning. Had it been said *all living creatures*? He must make sure.

Climbing the hill after mass he drew close to Vicente. "Papá—did
the padre say all creatures were to be brought, or did he particularly
say all living creatures?"

"Living creatures, to be sure. No one would bring a dead one."

"But did he say—living?"

"Did he say—did he say? Stop molesting me. The padre spoke
plainly enough for Rafael to understand."

In despair Paco dropped behind and walked beside his mother.
"Ma'mita—what did the padre say about the creatures? Were all to be
blessed?"

"All living creatures, yes. We will take one of each—a burro, a goat, a pig, a hen, and the turkey—that all may multiply well." Rosa nodded and smiled her contentment.

But Paco doggedly went on to another—to his brother Claudio. "Thou hast ears, muchacho. Thou canst hear the smallest sound the longest distance. What did the padre say about the creatures being blessed?"

"That they were to be blessed." And that was all Paco could get out of him.

Nombre de Dios! What was there left for him to do? He was being crushed between the words of the padre, spoken at mass, and a promise he had made the least one. Was it his fault—was it the least one's fault that he had become a wooden burro? Once he had been a very living creature—would not the good saint understand and give him his blessing even so? It was too perplexing. His mind became riled, turbulent as a muddied pool.

For all it was a gay dinner that Sunday, for all but Paco. Rosa promised such a fiesta as they had never known—enchiladas of chicken—sweet fruits—smoked sausage and a very special chile, rich with oil, fragrant with garlic. From her tongue and Vicente's came tales of other fiestas on the Day of San Francisco that they could remember: how the lame and the sick had been healed by the blessing; how the thrush belonging to Pepe, another carrier, had had its voice restored to it and had sung better than any other thrush until the day it had died; how the cows, blessed, had given birth in the spring to twin calves. Paco would have listened with delight had it not been for those words *living creatures* that stuck in his throat and strangled him.

He could not find breath even to laugh at the tale of Manual Juárez's

green and yellow parrot—the very one that now hung on its perch outside the sandal-maker's shop. She had been brought from Yucatán,
and once had sworn terrible oaths which had shocked the ears of all
passers-by. But after the blessing she had spoken only in English or
sung parts of a salve—never swearing again.

Words shuffled against Paco's ears like seeds in dried gourds—they
told him nothing. All he was capable of thinking about was this matter
of the blessing. It must be brought to pass for the least one. For two
days, outwardly, he did many things; inwardly he concerned himself
with ways of getting the burro into the cathedral gardens, with or
without Pedro's consent.

News of the fiesta spread as far as Mexico City and tourists began
arriving. Here was trade that Paco did not miss. He brought many to
buy sandals; he held many in the Zócalo to have their pictures taken
on the burrito more famous than nothing. There were so many coins to
tie into the tail of his lavender shirt that he could not sit down com-
fortably. He wore his most enchanting grin, but there was no grin
in his heart. The day before the fiesta was for Paco a day heavy with
silver and heavy with heart-ache. The sandal-maker, counting how
many sandals he had sold within the day, gave Paco a tostón and bade
him go celebrate as befitted a man of business.

Aí, if he but could! If he but had the wits to think a saint, a burro,
and a blessing together. No longer did he have to add money to the
combination. There was enough in the hidden gourd to set in motion
any one of the plans that he had made for himself and the least one.
Ehu! Merchants they could become in truth could the woodenness be
lifted from Chiquitico and his polished hoofs be freed of the board and
the wheels.

That night before the fiesta he had the cathedral to himself. Kneeling before the niche where many candles now burned, he groped frantically with his tongue for words. "Good San Francisco—very nice San Francisco—this is Paco—one of thy many name-children. To-morrow when the hour of vespers comes I supplicate thee to remember me and the least one. Thou knowest who I mean—the burrito of wood who now stands in the park, hearing nothing, seeing nothing, smelling nothing. It is for him now I pray. Save a little piece of thy blessing for him, good San Francisco!"

THE LEAST ONE COMES HOME

ON that day of early October the village was made gala with holiday crowds, music in the streets, sellers of tortillas and enchiladas in the Zócalo, tourists gabbling in strange tongues. And, after the noon hour, all shops were closed.

Rosa had washed an extra day at the estanque that she and Vicente and all the ups-and-downs might go resplendent. The creatures had been combed and cleaned and the little one of the burros had a garland of ash-berries around her neck.

Paco could eat no breakfast. A fresh lavender shirt on his back and his hair made to shine and lie down with much oil, his feet washed, but that was foolishness for they would be dusty again before oraciones; he set out, running, for the Zócalo.

He found Pedro rushed with trade, but, strangely enough, wearing a sullen expression.

"Aí, hombre, what ails thee?"

"It is that Consuela. Paco, I advise a man against marriage. It is beyond all thinking how much scolding a woman can do."

"Is that true!" By way of appeasement Paco looked astonished. In all things he must agree with Pedro. 'And is it permitted to ask what began the scolding?"

"A small black dog, of no size at all. A neighbor gave it out of a litter to Consuela last night. And now, with a day of fiesta at hand and money raining on me as if from heaven, she will agree to nothing but that I shall go with her in the procession and help her offer the creature for blessing."

"Qué lástima—what a pity!" Paco allowed his head to wag dolefully. Then he brightened. "This fiesta has not been celebrated for years. Who knows? . . ." He shrugged. "It is well, perhaps, in case it does not come again for many years to present oneself to the attention of the good saint. One never knows what blessings it may bring. And to keep peace between thyself and Consuela—that is something."

In the midst of much hurrying the photographer stopped to eye him with astonishment: "How dost thou come by so much wisdom? No—no—take up no time for the answer. I will finish this picture and then fetch Consuela and the pup. And thou shalt mind the camera and promise pictures for all with their creatures when the blessing is over."

As Pedro departed, Paco spun himself about like a top. He ducked from under his wide sombrero, caught it on the finger, sent it twirling aloft, and caught it upon his head. "I will mind all. I will see that everything is right. Who knows? Thou mayest sell that small black dog for a peso some day. Ohu, it is a good fiesta!" He shouted this after the vanishing figure of Pedro.

And then, suddenly, his legs began to bend under him like young bamboo sprouts. He had to sit down on one of the stone benches. Almost the moment had come. Almost this thing of which he had dreamed and whispered to the least one since he had been a few weeks old, this wonderful thing was about to happen. It filled him so full of fear and exaltation that his legs could no longer support him. Would he dare to wheel Chiquitico across to the garden and take his place in the procession?

Mid-afternoon and the village was choked with people and creatures. Down from the hills, along the roads, from near-by villages—men, women, children were pouring in. The air was full of bellowings and brayings, of whimperings, barkings, bleatings, and mewings. Ever so often the louder noises would suddenly hush and above all would soar the notes of some bird. "It is like the rumblings of the organ and then above it the music of the magnificat," thought Paco. "It is, maybe, the creatures' salve to San Francisco." His heart within him wrenched. There was the least one, close beside him, and he could utter no sound of glorification. If he had not been wooden and dumb, what a stupendous braying he would be making this minute!

Paco's eyes followed the procession now moving slowly within the cathedral gates. There was the son of the silversmith carrying his hairless dog, all eyes and ears and quiverings, and no bigger than a rat. There were the Potosi brothers, from a farm in the next valley, leading a fine young bull between them, his head garlanded with pink camellias. There was Doña Berta with her two lovebirds, the cage streaming with triple lengths of bright pink satin ribbon. There was the whole family of Ferreira—they made a procession in themselves. Juan carried a lamb, Pilar, his wife, a fine cockerel, and two by two came the children, leading between them a pig, a goat, a young calf, a burro blind in one eye. The family would acquire much blessing among them. They would need it, Paco thought, for they were not too kind to their creatures.

Paco's friend, Jesús Gonzales, with his sister, Tita, were bringing a home-made cage of willow with a wild linnet in it, who was making music sweeter than any angel. The little dun creature was singing his throat full, every note coming clear as a bell. "Sing, thou, sing!" Paco shouted at the top of his own voice. "Mayhap the saint will hear thee and bless all because of thy song."

There was a strange boy with a monkey, a tiny thing who clung in fright to the shirt of his small master and gibbered at the whole fiesta. Adelina, the youngest daughter of the sandal-maker, came bearing the parrot from Yucatán on his perch for a second blessing. She delighted the tourists by shouting in English: "There you come!" Paco laughed with them. It was good to forget for a moment how tremendously important this day, this very hour, was.

At five, en punto, the bells on the towers began their ringing. To-day they had words for Paco. To his ears they rang the usual: "Ding-dong-ding-dong," but to his heart they rang: "Come-come-come-come!" And he answered them in a whisper: "We come, absoluta-mente. Only we come at the end of all."

As the crowds jostled below him he remembered his obligation to Pedro and shouted, naming this one and that: "Remember Juan! Stop after the blessing. A picture of thee and the calf." Or it was: "Hola—Tomasino—a souvenir of the day. The little pig thou lead-est will photograph well."

But now the procession was nearing the cathedral door. Tongues quieted; a hush fell even on the animals. Those at the last crowded through the gates and spread themselves about the gardens that they might watch others until their turn came. What a crowd—what a fiesta! Paco sucked in his lips with excitement.

He became absorbed in everything—everything. For a while he forgot himself and the least one. The great doors of the cathedral had

been flung wide. Padre Anselmo had come out in all his finest vestments; two altar boys followed him, one with the bowl of holy water, one with the burning censer. Paco climbed the bench that he might see everything. Already the sharp, spicy odor of the burning incense filled the still air. The chanting of the blessing began. The censer was raised. The water was sprinkled. How quickly moved the hands of the padre; how gently they touched each living creature!

Each living creature! Paco drew in his breath and sighed it out with a fresh anguish. Now that he was seeing the blessing performed, now that it was actually taking place before his eyes, he knew how hopeless it would be to ask what he had to ask. Present the wooden burro which all had seen for half a year now, standing in the Zócalo, ask a blessing upon such an absurdity? Never! The padre would rebuke him; the crowd would jeer. No one would understand how right it was that the least one should have this, his only chance at becoming the living creature he once had been. No one would understand the promise, conveyed through the Blessed Mother to San Francisco.

Paco climbed down from the bench and buried his face in the burrito's saddle. How long the enormous sobs shook him he could never have told. His lashes were wet and he saw as in a blur that daylight was fast going, that the procession still filled the gardens, reaching to the gate. It would be dark before the blessings were all given. Pedro could take no more photographs this day. And by the time the last creature reached the cathedral door could the old padre tell whether it was living or wooden—whether it walked on its own four hoofs or whether it was wheeled? Was it not worth trying with dusk so close at hand?

Paco threw an arm about the neck of the least one and drew him quietly along, bending a little to whisper into one of the stiff ears: "Chiquitico, we go. If there is room in thy wooden inside for a prayer, make it now!"

Inch by inch, through the crowd he worked his way with the least one. All eyes were set ahead upon the procession, moving slowly forward. Paco clucked softly with satisfaction. He would go around the crowd, at its back, and no one would see. Inch by inch, inch by inch, he came at last to the great bougainvillaea vine, and looking not so much like a vine as like a great spreading tree. His eyes, searching, searching for cover, found a narrow, gaping emptiness between two of the hanging branches. Underneath, close to the trunk, there might be safe harborage for both of them until dark had come and the procession had neared its end. Then he would risk pulling Chiquitico up for the blessing. The padre's eyes were old; the altar boys even now were losing interest.

A yap-yap-yap broke the immediate stillness. Around the bougainvillaea came a figure. It was the son of the silversmith; it was the hairless dog which was yapping. Straight upon Paco and the least one they stumbled and Ignacio popped his eyes with suspicion.

"So—thou stealest what isn't thine?"

"I steal nothing."

"Son of a carrier, thou liest. Thou art running away with the photographer's burro while all are at the fiesta."

"I run away with nothing. I am taking care of the burro for Pedro while he has a better dog than thine to be blessed."

The son of the silversmith danced with madness, clutching the small shivering morsel without hair to his chest. "Say that again—I dare thee."

"I say it again—but with my fists. Ever since the two of us were born I have itched to punch thee. One on the nose, one on the chin, one in the stomach. They cost thee nothing." Paco dealt according to his word—not too hard but hard enough. "A better dog than thine—a better dog than thine—a better dog than thine!"

Too late did he understand that in satisfying the longing of a lifetime he had almost defeated his greatest wish and promise he had ever made. For the son of the silversmith backed from him and ran, weeping violently and shouting: "I will tell my father—the padre—every-one—that thou art a thief!"

Paco was stupefied by what he had done. He must hurry back at once to the Zócalo and restore the least one. Or he must hide. What good it would do him now to hide he had not the least idea. Por Dios! Anything but to go back. He parted the trailing, tangled vine of the bougainvillaea and pushed the least one ahead of him. Back of the curtain of leaves and blossoms there was an emptiness greater than he had imagined. It received not only the burrito but himself. Carefully he arranged the vine to cover their retreat, and with a heart that hammered inside of him like twenty mallets he curled up and laid his head on the least one's board. "Aí—we can breathe but we cannot see," he said.

After a little, when his heart had quieted, he began to feel the snug pleasantness of the hiding place. Who would find them there? Even now he could not abandon hope. In that crowd Ignacio could not move too fast; and were there not more compelling things to attend to at the moment than whether the photographer's burro had been stolen or not? Even yet he might gain the tail end of the procession and have the least one blessed before anything was discovered. What a strange thing was hope! It died in one like a fire, only to burst again into full flame if one but breathed a little on the embers.

He had slept not too much the night before. Now he was very sleepy. He yawned, turned over, thrust his head out between the sweeping vine and saw that two more altar boys had joined the others at the doorway. These bore lighted candles. Already pale stars were showing in the sky; and slowly, to the sound of braying, lowing, barking, the procession moved onwards.

"There must be still half a hundred. I have time to close my eyes while I count them; then I will look again." Paco pulled in his head, laid it gently upon the board, counted past twenty and was sound asleep.

He slept through the last of the blessings, through the departure of all, the closing of the great cathedral door, the ringing of the bells, the laughter, the shouting, the shaking of the earth beneath him under the tread of so many feet.

By the time Paco woke he had dreamed himself completely out of his skin. It was as if he had popped himself out, like a grape, and had seen a miracle performed.

Truly he had lead the least one to the doorway of the cathedral only to find it black, empty. Padre Anselmo had gone; the altar boys with basin and censer and candles had gone. Every living person, every living creature had gone, and night hung over all like the mantle of some Holy One.

And he had dreamed that as he stood there, lost, crushed, knowing not what to do, a voice spoke to him from the stone relief above the door. The voice was soft, singing, like a summer wind: "Paco—wait. I will bless thy burro for thee. Thou hast kept me reminded well and long of what thou hast set thy heart on."

And from the blackness had dropped San Francisco, somewhat mussed, but wholly smiling. But whether he had dropped from heaven or from the archway, Paco couldn't have told. It was enough that a fastening had given way somewhere, that the hand of the Holy One was resting at last on the head of the least one. Ohu, what a dream!

Paco thrust his head out from the tangle of hanging branches. It was night. That much was no dream. Nor was it a dream that all had gone,

that the village had emptied itself back into the houses, the farms, the near-by hamlets. Beyond him lay the cathedral—dark as a tomb.

He drew his head back and his hand thrust out in the more complete darkness of the bougainvillaea vine. Two hands began to grope—here, there—above, below. They could find nothing but hanging vines. No burro. Where he had rested his head was dry ground.

Suddenly Paco was frightened, frightened of the night, the emptiness the thing he had done, and the complete absence of the least one. Had the son of the silversmith told? Had he reported to the village that Paco was a thief? Had they come, even while he slept, and found them together? Was the least one even now restored to Pedro Villa, and resting on his wooden board under the thatch of his shed?

If this was the truth then here was the end of all! Aí, what good now to him was the silver put by in the gourd, hidden at the bottom of the barranca! What good were promises and prayers, lighted candles and the making of one magnificent pair of sandals! He would live and die a sandal-maker, with the stench of the goat-hides forever in his nostrils.

Paco felt his legs dead under him. They had no feeling. His heart had no feeling. His head was wooden, without sense of any kind. He stumbled out into the cathedral gardens. All about him was such a stillness, such a night-chill that he began to shiver. Not little shivers that went no deeper than one's skin, but great, shaking shivers that made him tremble all over from his belly outwards. He would like to throw himself into the very steepest of all the barrancas and die there.

But first he would go and tell San Francisco, aloud and with many words, what he thought of him. Not the inside saint, for the doors of the cathedral were closed and bolted, but the outside saint of stone; and he could tell what he chose to the inside one.

Down the well-trod path he walked, his feet moving uncertainly, his eyes so fastened to the stone archway that he saw nothing else. He would speak to the saint as man spoke to man, on his feet. It was no time for kneeling. He had made his supplications for months and it had done nothing for him but to brand him as a thief, here, before his own village, his papá, his mamá, and the ups-and-downs. He choked; he could not swallow, thinking of tomorrow and all the tomorrows.

"Listen, santo mío, listen! Already knowest thou what thou hast done—or left undone! ... "

He got no further. Something vigorous and insistent nudged him from behind. And before he could turn, a long, blasting bray shook the silence of the night and broke it. "All the Holy Ones in heaven protect me!" Paco whispered before he allowed his feet to spin him about. And even then he was afraid to look—to feel.

But there was a wet muzzle, there were four slender gray and white legs, with one gray fetlock and one white, behind; there was the nick in the right ear. It couldn't be. It was! There against the blackness of the night stood the least one, trembling all over even as Paco trembled. It was good to do nothing but to nuzzle close, to draw in many breaths and let them out in ecstasy, to feel and make certain all that his eyes saw was true.

"Ohu! Thou art flesh and bone and hair and sweet breath! Thou art the best and the most to be desired burro in all of Mexico, in the Atlantic and Pacific Oceans, in the United States of America, and in the whole world." Paco's arm curved tightly about the least one's neck. Boy and burro spun around that they might face again the stone archway overhead.

"There is thy saint and mine, and he has most wonderfully kept his promise. Kneel, Chiquitico! Each for himself shall tell the Holy One his sins and beg the penance may not be too heavy." Side by side they knelt, head of boy against head of burro. "But even if it is as heavy as the Pyramid of the Sun, our penance, we do not care, least one."

After such a day and night of fiesta, morning was far spent when the household of Vicente Rabell stirred. All were there, and Rosa was cooking the fresh tortillas for breakfast when it was discovered that outside the jacal stood three burros, the small one, the color of slate, the little one, brown as pottery, and the least one, of a soft gray-and-whiteness to delight the eye and heart. Rosa clapped her hands. "Look —he has come back to us! He must have wandered over the great mountains to be gone so long."

The ups-and-downs jumped up and down and shouted: "Aí—look, Paco! It is thy least one come home!"

Vicente did nothing and said nothing at all, only looked hard at Paco, who stood with his back against the papaya tree and looked at his father, shyly but steadily. "The least one has come home and he is mine." He spoke it as a truth and not as a question.

"He is thine, according to my promise, but both must work. You are not nurselings, the two of you, any longer."

"We are merchants. We will work, but in our own way!" Paco said it, not without pride and relief. No longer four walls and the stinking tubs of goat-hides for him.

It was amazing the wealth that the gourd held. Added to what had been tied only yesterday in the tail of the lavender shirt there was a fortune. At least enough for Paco's plan. He led the least one to the market and there carefully fitted two light baskets to his back. No need of a bridle. Had not words between them always been enough? Into the baskets went all the things women in far-off villages might need: needles and thread, ribbons and pins, powder, confetti and scent and dyes, with a dozen other things to tempt the eye.

He came back to show all to the family. "I am now a man of much property—which I will sell for money—which I will tie up in the shirt-tail and with it buy more property. The money will grow a little; the property will grow a little, until there is much of both." Around in his mind this widening circle moved. There was no end to it. It made a ravishing thought. Vicente was amazed and delighted. He clapped his son on the back. "Tomorrow thou wilt be gone. Thou shalt take with thee the best serape; the best is none too good for a merchant. Some day thou mayest have many burros."

"That is too many. One is enough." Paco's arm slid about the neck of the least one.

Rosa and the ups-and-downs could not keep still with their delight. They fingered everything, walking about the pair many times that nothing should be missed. "I will bake a sack of tortillas tonight so there will be food to carry," Rosa said. "Tomorrow, at the estanque, I will tell the women who come to wash about my son."

"Our son," corrected Vicente.

Next morning the family of Rabell was astir early. A great day lay ahead: a good day of carrying for Vicente, with talk along the way; of washing for Rosa, with pleasant gossip mixed with the rubbing and rinsing; of much boasting for the ups-and-downs. The cock flew to the ridge-pole and crowed long and lustily as Paco packed his wares, settled the baskets with great care that nothing should gall the sides of the least one. Then he made his good-bys.

He climbed by way of the goat-paths, up and over the western hill, making for a wagon road beyond. He had picked his destination—a village where he had friends. That would make a good beginning, and it was good also to leave behind the great motor highway.

Boy and burro fitted their pace well together. They went slowly—but not too slowly. About them towered the mountains. As the grade grew steeper, the air grew cooler, more bracing; there was a hint of frost to it. Ehu! The thick serape felt good over his shoulders. He would sing, to ease the bursting of his heart with so much contentment. He would sing the "Song of the Cockroach."

The mountains—far off—remained the same, towering, snow-capped. The forests, covering the foot-hills, remained the same. The golden dome of the sky at noonday grew no whit less or nearer. But the wagon road on which he had traveled twisted and climbed upwards to become a single thread of gold, washed in sunlight. And at last boy and burro became as small as black beetles upon the horizon, and the "Song of the Cockroach" became lost in the wind and sunlight.